The Christmas Camel

Uncle Clyde

BOOK THREE IN THE UNCLE CLYDE SERIES

The Christmas Camel

Nancy Winslow Parker

Dodd, Mead & Company · New York

To the Warrens—
Hap, Tricia, Tania, and Katherine

 · Distributed in Canada
by McClelland and Stewart Limited, Toronto
Manufactured in the United States of America
2 3 4 5 6 7 8 9 10

Library of Congress Cataloging in Publication Data

Parker, Nancy Winslow.
The Christmas camel.

Summary: For Christmas Charlie receives a camel
from the Holy Lands that possesses an enchanting
mysterious quality.
[1. Camels—Fiction. 2. Christmas—Fiction] I. Title.
PZ7.P2274Ch 1983 [E] 83-9045
ISBN 0-396-08220-3

Christmas Eve

Merry Christmas to Charlie from Uncle Clyde!

EGYPTAIR
احترس
جمل
داخلها
TWA
Rush - live cargo...
TO:
CHARLIE

In the spirit of Christmases past, I am sending you Fafa, a one-humped camel from the Holy Lands.

I bought this Mehari in Egypt at the famous Imbaba camel market of Cairo.

TO:
CHARLIE

The Mehari are legendary racing camels. They can be seen streaking across the yellow, shifting sands of the sun-baked desert.

Long ago they served heroically in the Camel Corps of the King's African Rifles.

Fafa eats bushes, shrubs, and scratchy plants.
She can go seventeen days without water.

A dried-out dromedary can drink ten buckets of water in ten minutes.

Camels are not easy to train. From nose to tufted tail you cannot find a more independent-minded beast.

There is a knack to getting one to stand up.

But with understanding, patience, and love, you can turn this "ship of the desert" into a great friend.

Believe me, Fafa is no ordinary camel.

I have sent you this particular high-bred dromedary
because she possesses a mysterious quality which
I find enchanting.

Ride her on soft ground, since sharp stones
will cut the tender pads on her feet.

One wonders how many great events these ages-old
woolly beasts have seen in their long lifetime
on this earth.

May Fafa bring
you joy at
Christmastime.

Love from Uncle Clyde

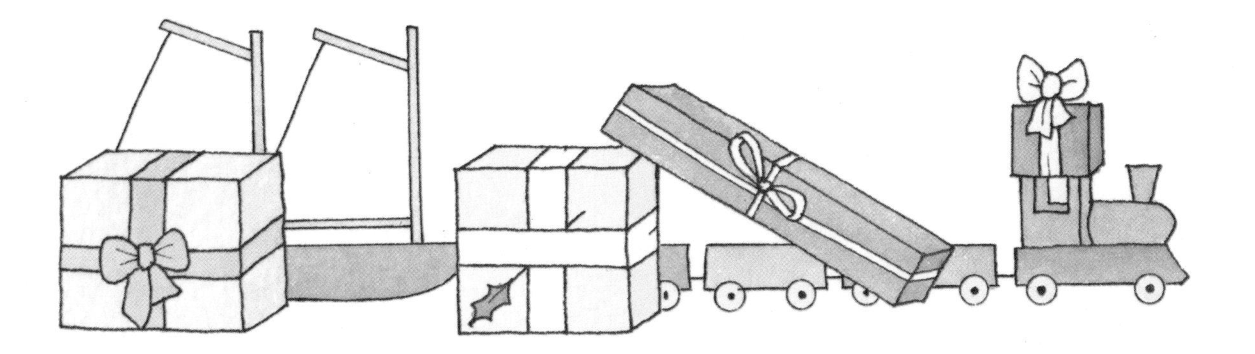